Published by Delacorte Press
Bantam Doubleday Dell Publishing Group, Inc.
666 Fifth Avenue, New York, New York 10103

First published in Great Britain by Julia MacRae Books,
a division of Walker Books Ltd., London

For Joan and Brian

The trademark Delacorte Press is registered in the U.S. Patent
and Trademark Office.

Library of Congress Cataloging-in-Publication Data
Maris, Ron.
Runaway rabbit / written and illustrated by Ron Maris. p. cm.
Summary: A runaway pet rabbit encounters dogs, a duck, and
other animals before eventually being recaptured by his master.
ISBN 0-385-29764-5
1. Rabbits—Juvenile fiction.   [1. Rabbits—Fiction.
2. Animals—Fiction.]   I. Title.
PZ10.3.M3225Ru   1989   88-23557
[E]—dc19   CIP
                                                 AC

Manufactured in Italy
First U.S.A. printing September 1989
10 9 8 7 6 5 4 3 2 1

Runaway
Rabbit

Ron Maris

Delacorte
Press

Where are you
going?

Into the house?

Into the pipc?   Yes . . .

. . . and out again!

Can I come in?

Where's Rabbit now?

Here's a carrot
for you.

Got you!

Don't run away
again, Rabbit.